Contents

Acknowledgment: Endpaper illustration by James Hodgson

First Edition

© LADYBIRD BOOKS LTD MCMLXXXIII

The Green Book of
bedtime stories

Ladybird Books
Loughborough

Just five sticks

by M E Snook
illustrated by Kate Lloyd-Jones

Once there were five sticks who lived together. The first stick was big and strong, and he loved to help. Whatever the others were doing, he would say, "Oh, do let me help you." They knew that they could always count on him.

The second stick was slender and rather mysterious. Sometimes when there was a boring or messy job to be done which nobody wanted to do, he would say, "Oh, leave it to me." And suddenly – the job would be done – yet nobody would have seen him DO anything.

The others would stare, puzzled and amazed. "How did you do that?" they would gasp, and the mysterious stick would grin happily. He loved to surprise them!

The third stick was not like the others. He was hollow and thin and a bit lazy and disagreeable. He didn't like doing his share of the work, and if one of the others told him to do something he would grumble "Oh blow!" And that wasn't very nice, was it?

The twins were small and neat, and very nice little sticks. They did everything together, and whatever they had to do they danced all the way to it and all the way back again.

One day the sticks made up their minds to go out and seek their fortunes.

"Oh blow!" said the hollow stick. He was so lazy that he did not want to bother, but the mysterious stick said, "Surely you don't want to stay here all by yourself? You would have to do *all* the work!"

"Oh blow!" said the hollow stick, but the strong stick said, "Come on, I'll help you." So they followed the others as they set off on the road to adventure.

When the five sticks reached a small town, they saw an old man walking along very slowly, one hand stretched behind to support his weak back, and the other stretched out in front to steady himself.

"Oh, let me help you!" cried the strong stick, and he leapt under the old man's outstretched hand.

"Why! You're just what I need!" exclaimed the old man, and with the stick supporting him, he walked quite well on his way.

The other sticks made their way around the market square.

"Oh blow!" muttered the hollow stick. He was cross because he no longer had the strong stick to lean on. Then he felt fingers closing around him, and someone lifting him up.

"Oh blow!" whispered the frightened hollow stick, and the man did − he blew right down through the stick!

"Ooh!" said the surprised stick.

"You'll make a fine pipe," said the man. He made some holes along the stick and blew again.

"That tickles!" cried the stick but his voice sounded quite different, and he giggled because it was fun.

The man kept on blowing. He blew songs to make the people sing, and jigs to make the people dance. The jigs made the twins dance better than they had ever danced before, and a drummer boy saw them.

"Aha!" he said. "You're just what I need for my drum."

He set their feet tapping on the drum skin, and the twins were delighted. They danced and danced on the drum, next to the piper.

After a while, the piper and the drummer took a rest and the crowd looked round for something else to do.

A tired old man was calling for their attention from the other side of the square. There was something about him which made the mysterious stick very interested.

"I have nothing up my sleeves," said the man flapping his sleeves to show that he spoke the truth. "And there is nothing in my hands," he said, showing his white hands with their long slender fingers.

"But now..." he raised one hand — but before he could drop his china egg into it, the crowd began to clap and cheer. Although they did not know it, the conjurer was just as surprised as they were, for there, in his raised hand, was the mysterious stick.

The looks of wonder and amazement on the faces of the people were just what the stick always loved and he was very pleased with himself. The astonishment in the eyes of the old conjurer pleased him most of all. He stayed and helped the old man all through the show. Together they pulled rabbits from hats, countless hankies from tin tubes, tore sheets of paper to shreds and made them appear whole again. At the end of the show the conjurer asked the stick to stay and help him with all the shows, and the mysterious stick said yes. This made the conjurer very happy, for his show had not gone so well for many a long day!

How happy the sticks were that they had gone to seek their fortunes! Now they were – a walking stick, drum sticks, a musical pipe, and a conjurer's wand. It was much more exciting than being just five sticks!

Colin the car

by Mary Hurt – *from an idea by* Neil Day
illustrated by James Hodgson

Colin was always dreaming. It helped to take his mind off the dirty rubbish dump around him. You see, Colin was a little red car. His owner had never looked after him very well, and when Colin started to rust and his tyres grew thin and smooth, he had been towed to the tip on the edge of town and left there.

Day-dreaming helped to pass the time for the little car, and it often brought a smile to Colin's face. Especially his favourite day-dream, when he dreamed that he was at the circus. When he closed his eyes, he thought he could smell the sawdust in the ring. He could hear the cheers of the crowd and the blare of the music as the ringmaster led the big parade around the ring. There were the elephants marching in time to the music, their trunks and tails entwined. He could see the acrobats in their spangled costumes, tumbling over one another as lightly as feathers. Then the lions with their tamer joined the parade. How fierce they looked, tossing their shaggy manes – but always obedient to the crack of the trainer's whip. Looking up, Colin would imagine the daring leaps of the trapeze artists as they flew through the air so gracefully and the crowd gasped with excitement.

Then a great wide grin would spread across Colin's face as he dreamed the best part of his dream. Here came the clowns, with their comical antics and their brightly coloured costumes. And, funniest of all — bow ties that spun round, and button-holes that squirted real water!

How Colin chuckled to himself as he imagined their tricks, and the shrieking and clapping of the children as buckets full of water were thrown about and the clowns went skidding and sliding around the ring. But then he would sigh. For, of course, all this was just a dream. How could he ever get to the circus from the top of a rubbish heap? Oh well, at least he could dream.

But one sunny day as Colin lay on the tip, he heard a strange rumbling noise which did not seem to be part of his dream. The noise grew louder and nearer, and as Colin peered over the top of the fence he saw a huge red lorry appear. Written on the side of the lorry were the words TOMLINS CIRCUS. He could not believe his eyes! A circus was coming to town! Behind the red lorry came a long line of other lorries, caravans and cages on wheels. Through the bars of the enormous cages Colin could see all kinds of animals – great grey elephants, fierce tigers and lions, velvety horses and slippery sea-lions. He shook himself to make sure it was not a dream. But it certainly was not. This was really happening.

Then from the cab of one of the lorries in the procession, two men appeared. They were looking in at the rubbish tip as if they wanted something in particular. Colin was puzzled as

the men poked and prodded around his buckled bumper, his smashed headlamps and rusty doors. Then they climbed back into their lorry, leaving Colin to wonder what it was all about.

The next day the little car was woken by the feeling of being lifted into the air. When he opened his eyes and looked around him, he found that he really *was* dangling in mid-air, on the end of a huge crane. The next minute he fell with a thud onto the back of a lorry, and was driven away from the dump. After a bumpy ride through the town Colin arrived in a large field on the other side of town. As he peered over the side of the lorry, he was surprised to see an enormous striped tent in the middle of the field. Nearby stood cages, some of them empty. The caravans of the circus folk stood a little distance away and people seemed to be busily preparing for the evening performance. He had been brought to the circus! But why? What could anyone possibly want with a little broken-down car like Colin?

After a few minutes Colin was taken off the back of the lorry and two men appeared in overalls. They were carrying a heavy box of tools. They stripped Colin of his twisted bumper, flat tyres and broken windscreen. Then they set to work with tins of paint, new tyres and spare parts. By the end of the afternoon Colin looked like a brand new car again. He could not believe it. And his excitement grew as one of the men got into the driver's seat, turned on the engine and with a loud brum-brum Colin set off across the field. This was too good to be true. He had been rescued from the tip and made to look like a new car again. But what for? Why did these men want Colin in the circus?

That night he found out. And can you guess what was about to happen to the little red car? The two men who had found him were really the circus clowns. They had been looking around for a car to use in their circus act, and Colin was lucky enough to have been chosen for the job!

As the band began to play, the clowns who were now in their costumes and with painted faces jumped into the little car. They drove into the circus ring with every spotlight shining on Colin's gleaming bumpers and glossy paintwork. The crowd cheered and laughed as the clowns whizzed around the ring beeping Colin's new horn and squirting water everywhere. Colin was so proud and happy that he thought he would burst. His dream had come true. He was the happiest little car in the world.

Judy - the little boat that never went to sea

by June Woodman
illustrated by Mike Ricketts

In a corner of the garden
Almost hidden by the flowers,
Propped up high on wooden blocks, poor
Judy sat for hours and hours.

She really was a very smart boat –
Painted, polished, bright and trim.
But her owner, Sam, was old now –
Boating was too much for him.

So, for two long years, our Judy
Leaned against the garden wall,
Dreaming of salt waves and wind, yet
Never put to sea at all.

Then one day in early autumn
Rolling storm clouds filled the sky.
Strong gales blew from off the sea and
Waves were lashed up, mountains high.

Still the shrieking winds blew stronger.
Fear now gripped the little town.
Wind, tide, storm all worked together
Sent the sea wall crashing down.

Water surged down every street and
Lapped the houses, row on row.
Folks found safety up in bedrooms –
But not those in a bungalow!

As Sam stood and watched the water
Rising over shoes and socks,
He began to shake and shiver.
Then, he heard some urgent knocks.

Over sounds of wind and weather
Louder still the knocking came.
As he peered through his front window
Sam gasped out dear Judy's name.

For that sturdy little boat had
Struggled till she floated free.
Now she waited, cool and calm, to
Rescue old Sam from the sea.

Bobbing down the road went Judy,
Bumping doors above the din.
Children, grown ups, dogs and cats cried
"Thank you!" as they scrambled in.

Judy's little upturned nose now
Headed for the higher ground.
There at last, at break of day, all
Were discovered, safe and sound.

Then, from near and far, reporters
Cameramen and crews all came –
Gathered round to pat brave Judy,
Who enjoyed her well-earned fame.

Now, if *YOU* should want to see her,
At the Boating Club she'll be.
They've made Sam the Commodore and
He's in charge of making tea.

In all weathers, wet or sunny,
Someone *ALWAYS* wants a ride.
From the Club House, gold braid shining,
Old Sam gazes out with pride.

So, each day now, little Judy
Sails out till the sun goes down.
Then she's tucked up, safe in harbour –
She's the *MASCOT* of the town.

The shining dragon

by Elaine Dalton
illustrated by June Jackson

"Now. Breathe out very slowly like this."

Dandy Dragon watched as two long jets of flame spurted from his father's broad nostrils. A big cloud of smoke curled around the castle walls. It was lesson time for the young dragons.

Dandy took a deep breath and blew very slowly. A very small smoke-ring crept out of each side of his nose. Not even *one* spark!

Dandy kept on trying, but he just couldn't make fire. All the other pupils were making showers of sparks. Red, blue, green, yellow and orange flames leapt all round the courtyard.

Soon the castle walls were hidden by the thick clouds of smoke. Dandy tiptoed away to the gardens to be by himself.

"Come along now!" He could hear Dreadnaught, his father, booming at the class. "The king and his court will be choosing their new gate-keepers tomorrow, and only the best of you will be chosen. That's much better, Donald! More flames and less smoke."

Dandy sighed as he listened. "No one will want *me* to live outside their castle," he thought.

He curled his long tail around his head, and hoped they would forget him when the competition started.

Dandy was a silvery-grey colour all over and rather small. He wished he was a handsome green like his friend Duncan or black and gold like his splendid father Dreadnaught.

The king and all the lords in Dragonara kept watch-dragons. They weren't needed to frighten away enemies – it was a very friendly country, but they were kept to welcome visitors.

Each year a grand competition was held to see which of the young dragons gave the best display, and the winner was chosen for the king's palace. The other lords picked the performers they liked best.

"You must look as smart as possible," fussed Dora Dragon, Dandy's mother, as she scrubbed his scales the next day. "I know you're the smallest, and you can't make fire yet, but someone may choose you if you look clean and smart. Don't fidget so."

Dora polished every scale until it shone, then sent him off to join the other contestants.

This year, there were five of them.

"You're the smallest, Dandy. Go to the end of the line." Dreadnaught puffed about importantly, talking to his pupils, watched by the king and all his lords and ladies. Sunshine

sparkled on the shiny scales of the excited young dragons, and on the brightly-coloured flags which fluttered around the edge of the big plain where the competition was to be held.

One by one each hopeful animal thumped to the middle of the ring to take his turn at breathing fire.

Dandy's friend Duncan was first. He blew fiercely. A line of silver-tipped blue flames ran backwards down his green scaly back, right to the tip of his tail.

"I'll take that one!" shouted the king. "I've never seen that before. I'll have him even if he isn't the winner."

"Watch me!" Donald Dragon's golden flames streaked out like forked lightning from his wide nostrils. He was soon chosen by one of the lords.

A bright blue youngster called Dermot sent out a stream of green sparks. Lord Hector wanted him.

David Dragon could only send out two straight red flames, but they went a very long way. All the lords and ladies had to move out of the way very quickly! He was chosen by Lady Arabella.

"Everybody's being chosen," Dandy thought sadly. "Even if they don't win, they'll have somewhere to go."

"Go on." Dreadnaught gave Dandy a push with his snout. The little dragon tripped over his own tail as he stumbled into the middle of the ring. He felt very foolish.

"It's only a little one. Not worth watching!" one of the ladies said loudly. She started to move away towards the tents where tea was being served.

"He's very pretty!" Dandy heard a little girl's voice say.

He felt a little braver. Taking a deep breath, just like his father had taught him, slowly he blew...

A very small puff of smoke trickled out of each nostril.

There was silence for a moment.

Then someone began to laugh. Soon all the company were laughing. Even the king had a slight smile on his face.

Then above the laughter an angry voice called, "Don't laugh at him! He tried very hard."

It was the little girl who had said he was pretty. She was called Fiona.

"Do give him another chance!" she begged the king.

Dandy hung his head in shame. He felt all his scales growing hot with embarrassment. He gave a shudder, trying not to cry.

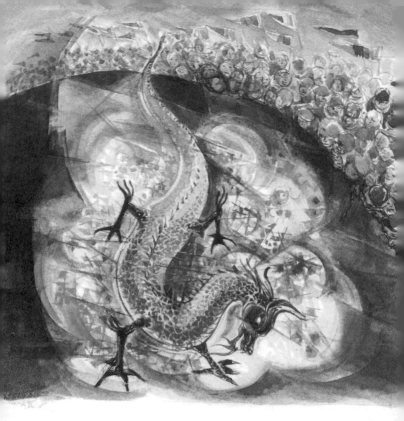

Then he gave a long, long sigh, and a cloud of multi-coloured lights flickered in front of his eyes.

The laughter died away.

In the silence Dandy gave an even greater sigh, and as he did so, his whole body glowed with a clear shining light. All the air around him lit up with lights of every colour. They flickered and danced about in ever-changing, glorious patterns of beauty.

"Ooooh!" Everyone else sighed – this time with pleasure. "Again! Again, Dandy!" they called.

The little grey dragon opened his eyes and looked at all the people through his tears.

He heaved an even bigger sigh of pleasure at all the happy faces — and glowed more brightly than ever. He looked down at his glowing feet and laughed happily.

"Please can we take him home? Oh please, Father, can we take him?" Fiona pleaded.

"We'll have to see if the king wants him," said her father, looking down at her. "You mustn't be disappointed if he wins. The king always takes the winner to the palace."

Fiona watched as the judges talked together, with the young dragons all lined up waiting. She wanted the little grey dragon to win — but she wanted to take him home herself!

At last the king stood up, and everyone turned towards him.

"The winner of this year's competition," he announced, "is the dragon Duncan. We have never seen such beautiful fire before."

They all clapped as the king placed a medal round Duncan's neck, but some people were surprised. They had thought Dandy would win.

"The young dragon Dandy gave us a most wonderful show, and I'm sure we would all like to have him at our castles, but we did not give him the prize because he is not a fire-breathing dragon. I hope he won't be disappointed," the king smiled at Dandy, "because we are very proud to think that Dragonara has produced the first shining dragon that any of us have ever seen."

Fiona tugged at her father's sleeve, and quickly he called out loudly that they wished to choose Dandy for their castle. There were many others who wished to have him too, but they were too late — Fiona was already leading Dandy away.

After that people came from all over the place to see the gate-keeper of Fiona's father's castle. The magnificent colours danced higher and higher in the air, always changing, always different. It was a wonderful sight at night-time to see Dandy aglow from the tip of his nose to the end of his tail and the marvellous patterns flickering in the sky, and no one ever wanted to go home until Dandy had gone to sleep.

When Fiona grew up, she married a prince, and Dandy led their wedding procession with the most fantastic display of lights that he had ever made. Then they all went to live in the prince's country.

Sometimes the sky at night in icy lands flickers and shines with wonderful lights. People call them the Merry Dancers, but perhaps — just perhaps — it could be Dandy, guarding Fiona's home, far, far away.

The other Joseph

by Wynter Weston
illustrated by Frank Humphris

Danny was very excited when Mummy came to fetch him from Play School. He ran to meet her, shouting, "I'm in the Christmas play, Mummy, I'm in the play!"

"That's very nice," said Mummy. "What are you going to be?"

"I'm the innkeeper," said Danny, "I have to say, 'No room, No room!' Mrs Timson says I'll have to wear a long robe and something tied round my head."

Danny was so excited he could hardly eat his tea. "Wait till I tell Daddy. He *will* be surprised, won't he!"

"Eat your tea," smiled Mummy. "Innkeepers can't do their work if they don't eat their food."

Danny told Daddy when he came home, and the next morning he told Peter the milkman, and the day after that he told Bill the postman. In fact, he told nearly everybody.

Each day at Play School, the children had to practise the play. There was a lot to learn, because as well as learning their parts, they had to learn the carols, too.

Mummy told Mrs Briggs, their next door neighbour, that Danny was singing morning, noon and night –

'Away in a manger, no crib for a bed,
The little Lord Jesus laid down His sweet head.'

One day Mrs Timson said, "We'll have to use the Wendy House for an inn. You'll have to sit down inside, Danny, and don't come out until you hear Joseph knocking." Then she looked round the room and said, "Now where on earth are those Three Kings?"

There was just enough room inside the Wendy House for Danny to sit on a small chair. Outside he could hear the shepherds talking, but he couldn't see them.

After a while, he found he could peep through the little window of the Wendy House and see the shepherds as well as hear them. He could see the entrance of the Three Kings, too. They were nearly always late coming in, and Mrs Timson sometimes got a bit cross.

"You Three Kings really *must* listen. You've been making far too much noise out there in the corridor. You must be ready to come in as soon as Judy has said, 'And there came Three Kings from the east.'"

"Mummy, what's a narrator?" asked Danny one day, when he came home.

"A narrator is someone who tells the story," she explained.

"That's what Judy is," said Danny. "She has ever such a lot of words to learn."

On the afternoon the dustmen came, Danny rushed to tell Joseph all about it. They were great friends, because Joseph always made time to listen to a small boy.

"I reckon you've got yourself a good part there with that innkeeper," he said. "It isn't too big, and yet it's very important."

"Do you really think so?" said Danny, looking quite proud.

"Of course I do. They wouldn't have had anywhere to sleep if it hadn't been for that innkeeper. Now would they?" said Joseph, as he fastened the front gate.

Danny couldn't wait to tell Daddy when he came home. "Joseph the dustman says the innkeeper was a very important man," he cried.

"Good for old Joseph!" said Daddy, smiling across the table at Mummy.

Each week the rehearsals got longer and longer, then a week before the concert, something awful happened. One of the Three Kings lost his crown. The kings had put their crowns in a large cardboard box along with their other things and somehow one of the crowns had been lost. Everyone had searched and searched, but it couldn't be found.

The Three Kings had been very upset, and Mrs Timson had promised that another crown would be made in time for the concert.

Then an exciting day came when Mrs Timson said, "Now, children, we are going to have a full dress rehearsal this morning. Everyone is to join in the singing, and you Three Kings be ready to come in when you hear Judy. Danny, you come out when Joseph knocks at your door. Right, let's begin."

Danny was so excited he could hardly sit still. He remembered to sing, and he could hear the shepherds. Then suddenly there was a loud knocking. Danny was very surprised, because it wasn't time for Joseph and Mary. He looked through the little window, and he couldn't believe his

31

eyes. Joseph the dustman was standing in the doorway. He walked over to their teacher and said, "Excuse me, Mrs Timson, but I just found this among the waste paper by the dustbins, and I thought it might be important."

There was a loud gasp when he held up the missing crown!

When Daddy heard the story that evening at teatime, he said, "Wasn't it nice to have a real live Joseph knocking at the door! I think next year, Mrs Timson will have to have a part for a dustman in the Christmas play. What do you think?"

Zebedee
the zany zebra

by J R Grainge
illustrated by James Hodgson

Out on the plains of Africa
One hot and sunny day,
Some little zebras, black and white,
Were busy at their play.

Their favourite game was hide and seek,
For they could safely pass
Unseen from tree to tree and still
Be hidden in the grass.

Young Zebedee, a daring lad,
(His mother called him Zeb),
Climbed to a cave and hid himself
Behind a spider's web.

None of his friends could find him there;
And, though they called his name,
Our Zeb stayed quiet and very still,
And so he won the game.

"I've won, I've won," he cried with joy.
"I always knew I would."
Then missed his footing − down he fell,
And landed with a thud.

The jungle creatures came to help;
A few were close to tears.
But Zeb jumped up and, with a laugh,
Said, "Do not worry, dears!

"I didn't hurt myself at all,
I'm perfectly all right."
"Oh no, you're not!" his friends all jeered.
"You look an awful sight."

For Zeb, on falling from the cave,
Had suffered such a fright,
He'd shattered all his lovely stripes
To squares of black and white.

"Oh, what a mess!" wailed poor old Zeb.
"Whatever shall I do?"
"Just go away!" his friends declared.
"We will not play with you."

A tear rolled down Zeb's chequered nose,
He felt so very sad.
His friends had all deserted him –
It really was too bad.

He wandered off to find a place
Where people wouldn't laugh.
The jungle beasts were most unkind –
Yes, even the giraffe!

He came, at last, into the town
Where people stood and stared
To see a zebra crossing by
All black and white and squared.

Then someone whispered in his ear,
"I know the place for you.
Come on with me, my strange young friend.
I'll take you to the Zoo."

The Zoo was just the place for Zeb.
The children loved his squares —
For noughts and crosses, chess and draughts,
They played all day in pairs.

And when Zeb's squares were all filled up,
He washed with might and main.
Then all the children gathered round,
To play on him again.

So Zeb has found his happiness
And now he's never blue.
He's playing games in black and white
All squared up at the Zoo.

The muddle day
celebration

by Prudence Blackwell
illustrated by Mike Ricketts

Everyone felt dull. Even the animals felt dull. They all wished that something exciting would happen.

"Something will come along," they said hopefully – but it didn't!

"We would like to celebrate," they said – but no one could think *what* to celebrate.

Days passed. The people felt duller and duller. Even the sun would not shine.

The postman sighed and said, "Oh dear," as he delivered his letters and parcels every day.

The baker sighed and said, "Oh dear," as he baked his bread and cakes and buns every day.

The bus driver felt very dull, driving along the same route every day. He almost forgot where the bus stops were. And the people in his bus sighed and said, "Oh dear."

Then one day Mr Thunkle, the mayor, had a good idea. He called together all the people of the town and said, "Let's have a Muddle Day."

Everyone was curious. "What happens on a Muddle Day?" they asked.

Mr Thunkle told them that on a Muddle Day everything was different.

No one had to do ordinary things.

People could change jobs for the day.

All the girls and boys could have a holiday from school.

Even the animals could make different noises.

And – there would be a big party in the Square. "Hooray," said everyone. "*Then* we won't feel dull."

They decided that the next Monday was going to be Muddle Day, and they started to get ready.

On Monday morning the sun shone brightly. Flags hung in the streets, and balloons bobbed from upstairs windows. In the Square there were long tables, covered with lots of good things to eat. No one felt dull.

"We are going to celebrate!" they said joyfully. And they did.

For a change, the postman delivered the milk.

For a change, the baker sold sausages and chops instead of bread and cakes.

For a change, the bus driver gave the children rides to the park in a pony and trap.

Everyone felt happy, and laughed a lot. Instead of doing what they *had* to do, they did what they felt like. The party in the Square went on all day long, and everybody sang a special Muddle Day song which Mr Thunkle had made up. It was a proper Muddle Day song, because it didn't rhyme at all!

The postman brought the milk
And the milkman brought the letters.
The baker sold the meat
And the butcher sold the bread.
It is our Muddle Day
And we are celebrating,
And everybody seems to be standing on their heads!

The cats started barking
The dogs started mooing,
The cows started neighing
And everybody said:
It is our Muddle Day
And we are celebrating,
And everybody seems to be standing on their heads!

Next day the people went back to their usual jobs.

The children went back to school.

The animals made their usual noises.

But no one minded.

"That's good!" said the postman, as he delivered his letters and parcels once more.

"That's good!" said the baker, as once again he baked his bread and cakes and buns.

The bus driver drove along his route in record time, and remembered where all the stops were. And the people in his bus said, "That's good!"

The people in the town decided to celebrate Muddle Day once every year, because it had made them feel so happy and cheerful again. Mr Thunkle, the mayor, was delighted too. Now everyone would always have something to look forward to.

No one need ever feel dull again!

Mandy
and the moon fairies

by Charlie Chester
illustrated by Hilary Jarvis

Although Mandy was only five, she was just about the proudest girl in the world. She had a secret, and she knew that if she told anyone, they wouldn't believe her. So she kept it to herself, but she smiled with pleasure every time she looked at her Fairy Tale Book. She knew that it had travelled further than any other book in the whole wide world. The strangest thing was, that although she had given it away, she had still got it, and here's how it all happened.

One summer night, after her mother had read a story about the fairies to her, Mandy looked at the pictures and turned the pages over for so long that she began to feel sleepy. Suddenly she heard the faintest little sound on the window ledge. As it was summer the window was open, and peering through the shadows Mandy saw the tiniest, sweetest little fairy you have ever seen. She stood there, like a butterfly, with wings that you could almost see through. She wore a little dress that shimmered in the moonlight, and she was really beautiful.

"Hello," said Mandy. "I was just off to sleep."

"Yes, I know you were," the fairy answered. "I have been sent to watch over you."

"Sent to watch over me?" asked Mandy.

"Yes, I'm Fairy Moonbeam. This is my work and I love it."

Mandy was puzzled for a moment. "If you have to watch over me while I sleep, when do you sleep yourself?"

The fairy laughed. "Oh, I sleep during the day. You see, I am a moon fairy and I only come out when the moon shines."

"I wish I was a moon fairy too," said Mandy. "I'd much rather come out like you do than have to go to sleep."

The little fairy thought for a moment. "Would you like to pay a visit to the moon fairies right up on the moon?" she asked.

"Oh yes, I would," said Mandy eagerly, and then she remembered to say, "Please."

The little Fairy Moonbeam smiled and said, "I'll take you to meet them all."

"How can we get there?" asked Mandy, a little anxiously.

"Oh, that's easy," replied Fairy Moonbeam. "All you have to do is hold my hand and you will fly with me."

Mandy hopped out of bed in a flash, and then she stopped. "Wait a minute," she cried. "I'd like to take the moon fairies a present. What can I give them?" She looked around for a moment. "Ah, that's it," she said. "I'll take them this book: it's got some lovely pictures in it and I'm sure they would like it!"

The moon fairy smiled. "I'm sure they will, and it was a very nice thought," she replied. "Come on now, hold my hand tightly and we'll be on our way."

Up and up they flew, far into the night, Mandy holding tightly to the moon fairy's hand. Higher and higher they went and Mandy noticed a very strange thing – the higher they went, the heavier the book became.

"We won't be long now," called the fairy. "We're nearly there." Soon they went through the billowy clouds, into the shadows and on into the night sky. "There it is. Do you see it?" shouted the fairy.

Mandy looked up and saw something very bright. "What is it?" she asked.

"That's the Milky Way," called back the fairy. Suddenly and very gently they landed on a bright star. It was all very quiet now and the fairy said, "There's no need to shout any more – we must whisper now."

"Why do we have to whisper now?" asked Mandy.

"I'll show you in a moment," she said. "But first, come and see the moon fairies at work."

They tiptoed along the star a little way, and then Mandy saw dozens and dozens of little moon fairies all working very hard.

They were polishing up the star to make it shine.

"My goodness," said Mandy. "I didn't know you had to polish up all the stars."

"Of course we do. We have to keep them all bright, and there are so many of them it takes us all our time. It's terribly hard work. What's more, we can only do it at night."

Mandy suddenly realised that with all the millions of stars in the sky, the moon fairies must spend their whole lives just polishing!

"Now then, are you ready?" the fairy suddenly whispered.

"Ready for what?" asked Mandy. She thought for a moment that the fairy was going to let her help with the polishing.

"Ready to see the day fairies — but we shall have to be very quiet and whisper," said Fairy Moonbeam. "You see, the day fairies have to work through the day, and they sleep at night."

"I see," said Mandy. "And you're a moon fairy, and you work through the night and sleep in the daytime."

"That's right," she said.

"Well, what do the day fairies have to do?" Mandy wanted to know.

The moon fairy laughed. "You'll see for yourself in a minute."

So saying, she took Mandy's hand and they flew towards a large, white, billowy cloud, all soft and silky. The moon fairy pushed the cloud gently and it seemed to open.

"Tiptoe in here, very quietly," she said.

Mandy followed her into the cloud — and what a sight greeted her eyes! The whole cloud had a silver lining, and it felt all soft.

"Don't let go of my hand or you will go through," whispered Fairy Moonbeam and then, as she gently lifted the second layer of the cloud, Mandy could see right inside. Rows and rows of tiny little deckchairs met her eyes, and in each little deckchair was a day fairy, fast asleep. At the foot of each deckchair was a tiny little pot of paint.

"Oh, aren't they sweet," said Mandy. "I never knew fairies went to sleep in the clouds."

"Oh yes, the day fairies do," the fairy told her. "These are day fairies, and their job is painting the rainbow during the day. Their job is a very big one, too."

"They must be very tired," said Mandy, "and we mustn't wake them, but I'm going to leave them a little present just to let them know that I've been here."

So saying she placed her book at the foot of one of the tiny little deckchairs. But, alas, the moment she let go of it, it disappeared from sight right through the clouds. It must have been too heavy...and here is the strangest part of all. The book that Mandy tried to leave as a present fell down towards the earth and then, when Mandy awoke the next morning, she found that, of all things, her book had landed in the very spot it had started from – right at the foot of her bed, where she had been reading it.

Maybe, if you are good too, one night the moon fairy may pay *you* a visit. She may even take you to see the fairies that paint the rainbow, and the fairies that polish the stars.

A kitten for Jane

by Mary Hurt
illustrated by Christine Owen

Jane could not believe her eyes when she came downstairs on her sixth birthday. There in the corner of the kitchen in a snug little basket was a tiny black kitten.

"Wh..where did this come from? Whose kitten is this?" she asked.

"It's for you. Happy birthday, darling!" said Mummy with a big smile.

Gently she lifted out the little furry creature who blinked and looked very timidly at Jane.

"For me?" whispered Jane. "Oh, he's lovely. But I thought Daddy always said we couldn't have a pet."

"Well, he's changed his mind, haven't you?" said Mummy, winking at Daddy.

"Yes," agreed Daddy. "You wanted one so much that Mummy persuaded me. But you will have to look after it."

"Oh yes. I will," said Jane, taking the little kitten from Mummy and stroking its soft head. She snuggled it cosily in the crook of her arm.

"Thank you," she said. "It's the best birthday present I've ever had."

"Well, let's hope it will behave itself," said Daddy, pretending to look very stern.

"I'm sure he will. He doesn't look too naughty, does he?" said Mummy. "You'll have to give him a name before long."

The kitten looked up at Jane again. It had such a comical little face that the name came to her immediately.

"I'd like to call him Scamp," cried Jane. "It really suits him. Don't you think so?"

"Let's hope he doesn't live up to his name then," laughed Daddy. "Now, how about seeing if the postman has brought anything this morning? It *is* your birthday, after all."

"Oh yes," squealed Jane. She had forgotten everything else in her excitement. She put Scamp carefully back in his basket and rushed to the front door. On the mat were quite a lot of cards and two parcels.

Jane carried them all back into the kitchen and hurriedly tore open the envelopes to look at her cards. Next came the parcels.

Mummy and Daddy had to help her to cut the string, and Jane was thrilled to find that Grandma and Grandad had sent her a beautiful wooden pencil box with a sliding lid and a top compartment that swivelled. It was filled with pencils of different colours, a rubber and a red pencil sharpener. And on the lid her name was printed in fancy letters. She would take that to school and feel very proud.

In the other parcel was a jigsaw from Aunty Pauline. And what do you think? The picture on the jigsaw was of two mischievous kittens peeping out of a basket almost the same as Scamp's. You see, everyone knew that Jane loved kittens. Aunty Pauline had chosen the jigsaw very carefully.

It was just then that Jane felt something soft against her leg.

It was Scamp. He had seen the string dangling from the table and could not resist it. He was playfully patting it with his paws. Next he pulled it right off the table and, rolling onto his back, he became completely entangled in the string. Jane laughed and laughed. So did Mummy and Daddy. They were going to have some fun with this little fellow, that was certain!

Mummy showed Jane how to make a little toy for Scamp. She rolled up a piece of newspaper and tied a length of string round it.

When Jane held the end of the string and jiggled the paper about on the floor, Scamp went mad with excitement. He pawed it and chased it all over the place. He crouched down low, watchfully waiting until it moved again. Then he pounced on it as if it were a mouse, rolling it over in his paws and tossing it up in the air to pounce on it again.

"I think it's time we gave that little kitten something to eat," said Mummy. "All that playing is going to make him hungry."

"Come on, Scamp," said Jane. "Ch..ch..ch," and she called her kitten over to where Mummy was pouring out a saucer of creamy milk. Scamp sniffed it suspiciously at first, but soon he was lapping it up, his little pink tongue flicking in and out as fast as could be.

When all the milk was gone Jane bent down and stroked her new little friend. Then she picked him up and scratched his furry head and chin. Scamp purred contentedly and snuggled up to Jane. And when she put him back into his basket, the little kitten curled up cosily, closed his eyes and fell fast asleep. He was worn out with all his play.

After breakfast, Jane skipped happily off to school. What a lot she would have to tell her teacher and friends this morning. This was her best birthday ever.

QUICK+ SIMPLE = DELICIOUS

Emily Kydd is a highly in-demand food stylist, recipe writer and cook. She lives in London with her partner Tom and greyhound Pearl and has styled the food for many cookbooks and various leading publications including *The Guardian*, *BBC Good Food Magazine*, *Olive Magazine*, *Jamie Magazine* and *Waitrose Food*. She has worked with lots of chefs and authors, including Tom Kerridge, Yotam Ottolenghi, Frances Quinn, Thomasina Miers, Antonio Carluccio and James Martin. Her recipes feature in several magazines and websites, and her first cookbook *Posh Toast* was published in August 2015.

Emily Kydd

QUICK+ SIMPLE = DELICIOUS

Genius hassle-free cooking

Photography by Louise Hagger

Kyle Books

For Tom

First published in Great Britain in 2016 by
Kyle Books, an imprint of Kyle Cathie Ltd
192–198 Vauxhall Bridge Road
London SW1V 1DX
general.enquiries@kylebooks.com
www.kylebooks.co.uk

10 9 8 7 6 5 4 3 2 1

ISBN 978 0 85783 361 7

Editor: Vicki Murrell
Designer: Caroline Clark
Photographer: Louise Hagger
Food Stylist: Emily Kydd
Prop Stylist: Alexander Breeze
Proofreader: Corinne Masciocchi
Production: Nic Jones and Gemma John

A Cataloguing in Publication record for this title is available from the British Library.

Colour reproduction by ALTA London
Printed and bound in China by 1010 International Printing Ltd.

good food doesn't have to be complicated

Everyone knows the feeling: it's been a long day, you're tired, hungry and staring at the supermarket or cupboard shelves wondering what on earth you can make for dinner. It needs to be quick, simple and, most importantly, delicious...

This collection of recipes is born out of this exact predicament. I'm a food stylist and recipe developer, which means that I spend most days, all day, cooking, which also means that the last thing I want to do in the evening is cook anything complicated. However, I also don't feel that the solution is an additive-packed ready meal (it goes against everything I believe in!) and so I started thinking about all the great dishes that can be achieved with just a handful of ingredients and minimum effort and still give you a tasty home-cooked meal on the table in no time at all.

What I discovered was that this approach doesn't restrict you at all – it's an advantage, giving you simple, unfussy cooking which, in my opinion, always tastes best anyway. So whether you're cooking for yourself, your partner or a crowd, the result is clean plates all round.

For a tasty weekend brunch for two, whip up the **avocado + maple bacon on toast** in only 15 minutes, or fix yourself a naughty **monte cristo sandwich**. If you make a batch of **mini frittatas**, the **kale + chickpea salad bowl** or the **chicken satay noodle bowl**, you'll have your work lunches sorted.

There are also plenty of options if you need to host a last-minute dinner party: try the **gnocchi + pistachio pesto** or the **cumin lamb with watercress + feta sauce**. Then for dessert, the **orange + passion fruit carpaccio** or **chocolate orange + avocado mousse**. And for something to serve with drinks, the **cheese + poppy seed biscuits** or **paprika chips + white bean dip** will go down a treat.

If your kids are keen cooks, they'll love making the **peanut butter + chocolate biscuits** and **no-cook chocolate cake**. In fact, everything is so simple, achievable and satisfying that every recipe is sure to become a firm favourite.

QUICK, SIMPLE, DELICIOUS

• Almost every recipe is designed to be ready in around 30 minutes, and they're all doable in under an hour. The 'ready in' time gives you the total prep, cooking and cooling/ chilling time for a recipe, but that doesn't always mean you'll be slaving away in the kitchen for all that time. Take the **chicken traybake sicilian-style** – it can be ready in about 1 hour, but 50 minutes of that hour it spends in the oven. And the **no-cook chocolate cake** spends most of its time in the fridge, leaving you free to enjoy a glass of wine, attend to the kids or get on with some life admin.

• There are no endless lists of ingredients. Every recipe has between three and seven main ingredients which are readily available and won't break the bank, plus a few storecupboard essentials that are listed on page 11. There are no complicated methods. The recipes can very easily be doubled, tripled, halved or quartered, depending on how many you're feeding.

• With classic combinations and new twists there's something for every taste and every time of day, from weekday lunches, weekend brunches and evening meals to snacks, treats and desserts.

maximum flavour, minimum effort

One of the keys to quick and tasty cooking is to use a few time-saving ingredients in the right places. Some people might call this cheating, but knowing when and where to take shortcuts and which ingredients to use means you can create delicious depth of flavour without spending hours in the kitchen – I call this intelligence!

For example, stirring some garlic and herb cream cheese into a pan of soft polenta adds bags of flavour in moments. Using spice pastes, mustards and chutneys are great ways to give dishes a boost. Stir a few tablespoons of mango chutney through some yogurt, and you have an instant salad dressing that will bring brightness to any plate. Or mash an avocado with a little wasabi paste or a hot horseradish sauce, and you have a super-quick side for a Japanese-inspired dish.

Take a good look at all the jars and packets and tins and pastes in your storecupboard and think how they can be incorporated into your cooking. And remember that some ingredients are beautifully versatile: one jar of peanut butter, for example, can be used to make a batch of tasty biscuits and a satay sauce to drizzle over a chicken salad.

To save time and effort, pre-cooked packets of rice, pulses and grains are brilliant. With a long shelf life, they're great to have in the cupboard when you need to whip up a speedy lunch or dinner (and of course, if you do have the time, you can also cook them from scratch – substitute 100g cooked rice for 40g dried rice and cook according to the packet instructions).

Ready-toasted and chopped nuts and pre-chopped vegetables will save effort in the kitchen without compromising on flavour, as will tinned beans and pulses. Sometimes life's too short to make your own pastry, and the ready-rolled stuff even saves getting the rolling pin out too.

Use herbs in abundance as they'll add lots of flavour and freshness. To help them last for longer (don't let them fester in the fridge!), wrap in damp kitchen paper and seal in a plastic food bag.

When cooking simply it is important to use the best possible ingredients you can find or afford, as this really will give you the best results. Most of the ingredients used in these recipes are readily available, and for things that may be harder to find there are recipe tips for what to use in their place.

storecupboard + fridge essentials

The recipes in this book only call for a handful of main ingredients but they do also require a few very basic, staple ingredients that are almost always on hand in any home kitchen. However, as it's always annoying when you start to cook and then realise that you're missing something rather essential to the method, here's a checklist of all the items that I assume you will have on hand to use as and when required:

in the storecupboard:

sunflower oil*

olive oil

extra virgin olive oil

white wine vinegar

balsamic vinegar

caster sugar

plain flour

self-raising flour

salt

pepper

* When a recipe calls for oil, use sunflower oil unless otherwise stated.

in the fridge:

milk

unsalted butter

a note on quantities and sizes:

a small bunch of herbs is 25–30g

½ small bunch of herbs is 15g

eggs are medium unless otherwise stated

1 tbsp = 15ml

1 tsp = 5ml

kitchen equipment

Cooking isn't just about the ingredients. Every kitchen needs a few basic but very key tools of the trade that will help all your efforts run that much more smoothly. Again, these are staple things that very few kitchens are without, but I thought it might be useful to supply another checklist so you can ensure you have exactly what you need:

chopping board

good sharp knife

wooden spoon

grater (with zester or a separate zester)

small, medium and large saucepans with lids

large non-stick frying pan

rolling pin

mixing bowls

measuring spoons

measuring jug

ramekins

sieve

spatula

balloon whisk

12-hole non-stick muffin tray

baking tray

roasting dish/tray

baking parchment

pastry brush

steamer – or use a sieve or colander suspended over a pan of simmering water

wire cooling rack

food processor (a few recipes call for one but it's not an essential piece of kit)

1.
BRUNCH
+ LUNCH

tarragon + red pepper baked eggs

serves 4
ready in 25 minutes

Heat the oven to 180°C/160°C fan/gas mark 4. Lightly butter 4 small ramekins and place in a roasting tray. Thinly slice **150g roasted red peppers** and pat dry with kitchen paper, then roughly chop a **small handful of tarragon leaves**.

Generously season **175g crème fraîche**, stir very gently, then spoon 1 tbsp into each ramekin, followed by half the red pepper and some tarragon. Crack **4 eggs** into the ramekins, one in each, and top with the remaining crème fraîche, peppers and tarragon.

Pour boiling water into the roasting tray so that it comes halfway up the sides of the ramekins and bake for 18–20 minutes until the egg is set to your liking. Grind over some black pepper and serve with lots of hot **toast**.

smashed potato cakes with smoked salmon

serves 2
ready in 45 minutes

Boil **4 small–medium Charlotte potatoes (about 85g each)** in salted water for 25 minutes, or until cooked through, then drain. When cool, squash each potato between the palms of your hands into roughly round patties, squeezing together tightly so they hold their shape.

Melt a generous knob of butter in a non-stick frying pan over a medium heat and cook the cakes for 3–4 minutes on each side, turning carefully, until browned.

Divide between two plates and top with **100g smoked salmon**, a **dollop of crème fraîche**, a **few snipped chives** and a grinding of black pepper.

Tip: Cook the potatoes the night before, then simply squash and fry to serve. If your potatoes are on the small side, boil 340g smaller Charlotte potatoes and squash several together to make each cake.

avocado + maple bacon on toast

serves 2
ready in 15 minutes

Dice **4 rashers of smoked bacon** and add to a cold frying pan with a little drizzle of olive oil. Fry, stirring, over a medium–high heat for 8–10 minutes, or until crispy.

Meanwhile, scoop the flesh from **1 extra large or 2 small avocados** and mash with a **squeeze of lime juice** and some seasoning.

Toast **2 large slices of sourdough bread** and top with the avocado mix. Stir **2 tbsp maple syrup** through the bacon in the frying pan and let it bubble for 1 minute, then spoon this over the avocado. Serve with lime wedges.

scrambled egg tacos

serves 4
ready in 15 minutes

Warm **4 taco shells** according to the packet instructions. Heat 2 tsp olive oil in a non-stick frying pan over a medium heat, add **1 finely chopped red onion** and cook gently for 4–5 minutes.

Lightly beat together **5 eggs** and season. Tip the eggs into the pan with the onion, wait 30 seconds and then stir, then wait another 30 seconds and stir again. Continue until the eggs are almost cooked, then stir through **85g quartered cherry tomatoes, 2 tsp chopped jalapeños from a jar** and **½ small bunch of roughly chopped coriander**.

Pile the scrambled egg into the taco shells and top with a **dollop of soured cream** and a **scattering of coriander**. Serve with extra jalapeños and soured cream.

Tip: If you can't find taco shells, brush 4 small corn or flour tortillas with oil and bake in the oven at 180°C/160°C fan/gas mark 4, or grill on both sides until golden brown and then top with scrambled egg.

monte cristo sandwich

serves 1
ready in 15 minutes

Beat **1 egg**, 2 tbsp milk and some seasoning together in a shallow bowl.

Spread **2 slices of bread** with ½ **tsp Dijon mustard** on each. Top one slice with **50g smoked ham slices** and **40g grated Gruyère cheese** and finish with the second slice of bread, mustard-side down. Slide the sandwich into the egg mixture and turn over gently until all the egg mix has soaked in.

Melt a knob of butter in a frying pan over a medium heat and fry the sandwich for 3–4 minutes on each side until the bread is golden brown and the cheese has melted.

Cut the sandwich in half, dust with a little **icing sugar** and serve with **redcurrant**, **lingonberry** or **cranberry jelly or jam**.

mini pea + spinach frittatas

makes 12
ready in 35 minutes

Heat the oven to 180°C/160°C fan/gas mark 4 and thoroughly grease a 12-hole non-stick muffin tin with butter.

Tip **100g spinach** into a colander and pour over a just-boiled kettle. When cool enough to handle, squeeze out the water and roughly chop.

Beat together **8 large eggs** with 100ml milk, **1½ tsp dried mint** and some seasoning. Stir through the spinach, **100g defrosted frozen peas**, **6 sliced spring onions** and **125g feta cheese**, roughly crumbled.

Pour the mixture into the tins and bake for 20–25 minutes until golden and set. Leave to cool in the tins a little before turning out.

baked ricotta + jammy tomatoes

serves 3–4
ready in 45 minutes

Heat the oven to 200°C/180°C fan/gas mark 6. Drain any liquid from a **250g pot of good-quality ricotta cheese**, then turn out into a small baking dish. Spoon over 1 tbsp extra virgin olive oil, season well and sprinkle over the leaves from **3 sprigs of thyme**.

Cut **5 small vine tomatoes** in half and lay cut-side up around the cheese. Drizzle ½ tbsp extra virgin olive oil and 1 tsp balsamic vinegar over the tomatoes and season.

Roast for 40–50 minutes, or until the cheese is golden and the tomatoes are caramelised. Serve with **slices of toast** and some **salad leaves**.

griddled nectarine, mozzarella + salami salad

serves 4
ready in 20 minutes

Heat the oven to 200°C/180°C fan/gas mark 6. Space out **12 slices of milano salami (about 60g)** on a baking tray lined with parchment paper and bake for 15 minutes, then leave to cool and crisp.

Half **3 nectarines**, remove the stones, then cut each half into three wedges. Heat a griddle or dry frying pan over a high heat and cook the wedges for about 2 minutes on each side until a little charred.

Tear **200g mozzarella cheese** into chunks. Arrange the nectarines and mozzarella on a large serving plate. Snap the salami into pieces and scatter over the salad, then drizzle with 2 tsp extra virgin olive oil and 1–2 tsp balsamic vinegar. Scatter over a **handful of basil leaves** and serve with crusty bread.

tuna grater
box salad

serves 2
ready in 15 minutes

Bring a small pan of water to the boil, lower in **1 egg** and simmer for
9 minutes. When cooked, drain, run under cold water until cool, then peel.

Meanwhile, mix **2 heaped tbsp mayonnaise** with **1½ tsp chopped dill**,
1 tbsp cold water and some black pepper.

Grate **1 large raw peeled beetroot (about 125g)** and divide between
two bowls, then grate **1 apple**, discarding the core, and add to the
bowls. Drain **1 tin of tuna (120g drained weight)**, and use a fork to flake
between the bowls, then grate over the egg, drizzle over the dressing and
scatter with **2 heaped tsp drained capers** and **a few sprigs of dill**.

Tip: If not eating straight away, toss the apple in a little lemon juice to
stop it going brown.

broccoli, halloumi + mango salad

serves 3–4
ready in 20 minutes

Bring a pan of water to the boil. Trim the stalk from a **400g head of broccoli** and break into florets, then simmer for 2–3 minutes until tender but still crunchy. Drain and set aside.

Drain a **400g tin of brown lentils** and tip into a bowl. Stir in ½ **finely chopped red onion**, the warm broccoli and some seasoning.

In a separate bowl, mix together **85g Greek yogurt**, **50g mango chutney** and 1–2 tbsp cold water to get a drizzling-consistency dressing.

Heat a large non-stick frying pan over a medium–high heat. Slice a **250g block of halloumi cheese** into 12 pieces and dry-fry for 1–2 minutes on each side until golden brown but still soft – you may need to do this in batches.

Divide the salad between plates, top with the halloumi, drizzle over the dressing, grind over some black pepper and serve.

coriander, roasted beetroot, goat's cheese + orange salad

serves 4–6
ready in 45 minutes

Heat the oven to 200°C/180°C/gas mark 6. Trim a **500g bunch of beetroot with leaves**, reserving the leaves and stalks, and cut into wedges. Toss with 1½ tbsp olive oil and **1 tbsp crushed coriander seeds**, then season, tip onto a baking tray and roast for about 35 minutes until tender, then cool.

Meanwhile, mix together **150g soft goat's cheese**, the **zest of ½ orange** and some seasoning, then set aside. In a jar, combine the **zest and juice of ½ orange**, 1½ tbsp extra virgin olive oil, **1 tbsp sherry vinegar**, then season and shake well.

Heat **250g pre-cooked grains**, such as spelt, according to the packet instructions, then tip into a bowl and leave to cool. Wash and roughly chop most of the beetroot stalks and add to the bowl, along with a few handfuls of leaves, washed and torn in half, then stir through the roasted beetroot and dressing.

Cut the end off the remaining ½ zested orange, then work a sharp knife down the outside to remove the skin and pith completely and cut the flesh into thin slices. Repeat with another **whole orange**.

Spread the goat's cheese onto a large serving plate and top with the grains and beetroot, then snuggle in the orange pieces.

kale + chickpea salad bowl

serves 4
ready in 20 minutes

Drain a **400g tin of chickpeas**. Heat 1 tbsp oil in a non-stick frying pan, add the chickpeas and a pinch of salt, and fry, stirring occasionally, for 10 minutes until crisp. Set aside.

Meanwhile, make the dressing: whisk together 3 tbsp extra virgin olive oil, 1 tbsp balsamic vinegar and plenty of seasoning in a small bowl. Add **50g blueberries** and roughly mash together.

Tip **150g washed chopped kale** into a large bowl, removing any tough stalks (125g after destalking). Add 3 tbsp of the dressing and, using your hands, massage well into the kale to soften. Add **1 extra large or 2 small chopped avocados**, the crispy chickpeas, **125g feta cheese** broken into chunks and **50g blueberries**. Lightly toss everything together, then drizzle over the remaining dressing.

tricolour chicken salad

serves 6–8
ready in 20 minutes

Whisk together 4 tbsp extra virgin olive oil, 1½ tbsp white wine vinegar, **1½ tsp Dijon mustard** and some seasoning.

Cut **2 Little Gem lettuces** into wedges and arrange on a large platter. Halve **1 cucumber** lengthways and use a spoon to scoop out the seeds, then slice chunkily on the diagonal and scatter over the plate.

Remove all the meat from **1 whole small ready-roasted chicken**, shred into large chunks and add it to the salad too.

Cut **2 small avocados** into thin wedges, then peel off the skin and scatter over the salad, along with **175g halved red grapes**. Shave over **25g Parmesan cheese (optional)**, and serve the dressing alongside.

salmon + sesame salad

serves 2–3
ready in 15 minutes

Heat **250g microwaveable brown rice or quinoa** according to the packet instructions, then leave to cool.

Meanwhile, grate **1 medium carrot** and peel ¼ **small cucumber** into ribbons. In a small bowl, mix together **1 tbsp sesame oil** and **1½ tbsp soy sauce**. In a dry frying pan, toast **1½ tbsp sesame seeds**, shaking until golden brown.

Toss half the sesame seeds and most of the sauce through the rice, then divide between plates. Top with the carrot and cucumber, then flake over **150g hot smoked salmon** and finish with the remaining dressing and sesame seeds.

avocado + spinach quesadilla

serves 1
ready in 10 minutes

Lay **2 mini flour tortilla** on your work surface. Mash ½ **avocado** and spread over one tortilla, then top with **50g sliced mature Cheddar or Emmental cheese** and **20g baby spinach leaves**.

Spread **1 tbsp tomato chilli chutney** (or your favourite kind) on the other tortilla and sandwich together. Brush the uppermost side with oil and cook, oil-side down, in a dry frying pan over a medium heat for about 2 minutes. Brush the top tortilla with oil, then flip over and cook on the other side until golden and the cheese has melted.

Tip: Use 1 large tortilla instead of 2 small; brush one side with oil, flip over and place the filling on one half and the chutney on the other, then fold in half and cook.

blue cheese + pear tarts

serves 6
ready in 35 minutes

Heat the oven to 220°C/200°C fan/gas mark 7. Unroll **320g ready-rolled puff pastry** and cut into six pieces, then place on a parchment-lined baking tray. Score a 1cm border around the edge of each pastry square/rectangle, making sure you don't cut all the way through. Bake for 15 minutes.

Turn the oven down to 200°C/180°C fan/gas mark 6 and, using a spoon, push down the centre of each piece of pastry. Arrange **2 sliced pears** over the tops of the tarts, crumble over **100g blue cheese** and **35g chopped walnuts**. Drizzle with a little olive oil and bake for 10 minutes.

Mix together 2½ tbsp extra virgin olive oil, **1 tbsp sherry vinegar**, **2 tsp runny honey** and some seasoning. Toss **150g crispy salad leaves** with some of the dressing and serve with the tarts. Drizzle the remaining dressing over the tarts.

tikka masala fishcakes

serves 2
ready in 20 minutes

Tip **175g skinless and boneless white fish fillets** into a food processor. Add **1 heaped tbsp tikka masala spice paste**, **1 egg white** and some black pepper and whiz until smooth, then shape into 8–10 patties.

Heat a shallow layer of oil in a non-stick frying pan over a medium–high heat. Cook the patties in batches for 1½–2 minutes on each side – don't worry if they stick a little – just scrape the crispy bits from the bottom of the pan and serve these too.

Warm **2 chapatis** in a dry frying pan, then transfer to a board or plate. Spoon **2 heaped tbsp raita or tzatziki** over each chapati, then top with a **handful of soft lettuce leaves**, the fishcakes and ¼ **sliced red onion**.

Serve with **lemon wedges** for squeezing over. Roll up like a wrap to eat.

2.
DINNER

cauliflower cheese steaks + parsley salad

serves 2
ready in 30 minutes

Heat the oven to 200°C/180°C fan/gas mark 6. Trim **1 small cauliflower** and slice it into 2.5cm steaks – you should have at least four. Place on a baking tray, brush all over with 2 tbsp olive oil and season. Roast for 20 minutes, then turn over and roast for 10 minutes more until tender and golden.

Meanwhile, mix together ½ **small bunch of roughly chopped parsley**, ¼ **finely chopped red onion** and **1 tbsp drained capers**.

In a pan over a very low heat, gently warm **100g crème fraîche** together with **40g finely grated Parmesan cheese** and some seasoning, stirring until melted and smooth (do not boil).

Divide the steaks between two plates, pour over the sauce and top with the parsley salad. Serve with **crusty bread** and butter.

**stuffed peppers
mexican-style**

serves 2
ready in 40 minutes

Heat the oven to 200°C/180°C fan/gas mark 6. Halve **2 red or yellow peppers**, remove the core and seeds, and place on a roasting tray. Scatter **1 sliced garlic clove** between the four halves, drizzle with olive oil, season and roast for 25 minutes.

Meanwhile, heat 1 tbsp olive oil in a frying pan over a medium–high heat. Drain a **400g tin of black beans** and tip into the pan. Add **1 tsp ground cumin**, **1 sliced garlic clove** and a pinch of salt and cook for about 6 minutes, stirring, until beginning to crisp.

Pile the beans into the peppers, crumble over **75g feta cheese**, drizzle with a little olive oil and roast for a further 10 minutes. Serve with **Mexican chilli sauce** and **1 small bunch of coriander**, roughly torn between the plates.

pumpkin, sage + goat's cheese frittata

serves 4
ready in 40 minutes

Spoon 1 tbsp oil into a large non-stick frying pan over a medium heat. Add a **350–400g packet of sliced or cubed squash (or squash and sweet potato)** and lightly brown for 2–3 minutes, then splash in 1 tbsp cold water, season, cover and cook for 8–10 minutes until just tender. Add 1 tbsp oil to the pan, tip in **1 large sliced red onion** and cook, uncovered, for 5 minutes, then stir in **2 grated garlic cloves**.

Whisk together **10 eggs**, **6 finely chopped sage leaves**, ½ of a **150g pot of soft goat's cheese** and plenty of seasoning. Pour over the veg in the pan, turn down the heat to its lowest setting and cook gently for 15 minutes, until nearly set.

Heat the grill. Dollop small spoons of the remaining cheese over the surface of the frittata. Mix **8 sage leaves** with 1 tsp olive oil and arrange on top, then pop under the grill for 2–3 minutes until golden and set.

creamy polenta + soft leeks

serves 4
ready in 15 minutes

Heat 1½ tbsp olive oil in a large frying pan. Add **4 medium–large sliced leeks**, 2 tbsp cold water and some seasoning, then cover and cook gently for 10 minutes until softened but holding their shape.

Meanwhile, cook **200g quick-cook polenta** according to the packet instructions, adding more water if necessary so that it has a porridge-like consistency, then beat in **170g soft cheese with garlic and herbs**.

Add **150g defrosted frozen peas** and the leaves from **3 sprigs of thyme** to the leeks and cook, uncovered, for 2 minutes.

Divide the polenta between bowls and spoon over the leeks. Grate over plenty of **Parmesan cheese** and sprinkle with a few extra thyme leaves.

stuffed tomatoes
provençal-style

serves 4
ready in 55 minutes

Heat the oven to 220°C/200°C fan/gas mark 7. Slice the tops off **8 large tomatoes**, scoop out the centre, drain this flesh in a sieve, then roughly chop.

Slit the skins of **4 pork sausages (about 285g)** and transfer the meat to a bowl, discarding the skins. Mix with the chopped tomato flesh, **1 small finely chopped red onion, 2 finely chopped garlic cloves, 35g breadcrumbs, a large handful of mint leaves, finely chopped** and some seasoning.

Stuff the mixture into the tomato shells, pushing down with the back of a spoon, then pop on the lids and fit snugly into a baking dish. Drizzle over 3 tbsp olive oil and bake for 40 minutes, basting halfway through the cooking time. Scatter with mint leaves and serve with a **leafy salad**.

roasted courgette + lentil salad with horseradish dressing

serves 4
ready in 35 minutes

Heat the oven to 200°C/180°C fan/gas mark 6. Slice **500g courgettes** on the diagonal into 1cm thick slices and chop **2 red onions** into 3cm chunks. Tip the vegetables into a roasting tray and toss with 2 tbsp olive oil, **1 clove of crushed garlic** and some seasoning, then spread out and roast for 30–35 minutes until caramelised, turning halfway through.

Meanwhile, mix **75g soured cream** with 1½ tbsp creamed horseradish sauce. Heat **500g pre-cooked puy lentils** according to the packet instructions, then toss with **100g baby spinach**, season and divide between plates. Pile the vegetables on top and dollop over the dressing.

Tip: If you can't find pre-cooked puy lentils, cook 250g dried puy lentils according to packet instructions.

herby rice with smoky prawns + peppers

serves 2
ready in 20 minutes

Thinly slice **1 red** and **1 yellow pepper**. Heat 1 tbsp olive oil in a frying pan over medium–high heat, add the peppers and some salt, and cook for 10–12 minutes until softened and starting to brown. Add another 1 tbsp olive oil to the pan and stir in **2 large finely chopped garlic cloves** and **1 tsp sweet smoked paprika**. Cook for 1 minute, then stir in **150g cooked and peeled king or tiger prawns** and warm through for 1–2 minutes.

Meanwhile, heat a **250g packet of microwaveable brown basmati rice** according to the packet instructions. Stir **1 small bunch of finely chopped parsley** through the rice and season, then divide between plates. Spoon over the prawns and peppers, then grate over a **little lemon zest** and serve with wedges from the zested lemon.

Tip: If you can't find microwaveable rice, cook 100g dried brown basmati rice according to the packet instructions. You'll need to do this first.

chorizo + courgette carbonara

serves 4
ready in 25 minutes

Bring a large pan of salted water to the boil. Heat 1 tbsp olive oil in a large frying pan, add **200g cubed chorizo** and cook for 3–4 minutes over a medium heat, then turn up the heat, tip in **350g grated courgettes** and cook for 6–8 minutes.

Meanwhile, boil **350g linguine** according to the packet instructions. Drain, reserving a cup of the cooking water, then tip the pasta into the courgette pan and stir.

Beat together **3 large egg yolks**, **75g grated Parmesan cheese**, the **zest of ½ lemon** and plenty of seasoning. Remove the pan from the heat and stir through the egg mix until thickened. Add 6–8 tbsp of the reserved cooking water and stir until the sauce is creamy. Serve with extra grated Parmesan.

gnocchi + pistachio pesto

serves 2–3
ready in 15 minutes

Bring a large pan of salted water to the boil. Toast **50g pistachio nuts** in a dry frying pan until browned, then tip the nuts into a food processor with **1 small bunch of parsley, 1 finely chopped garlic clove**, 4 tbsp extra virgin olive oil and plenty of seasoning. Whiz to a paste and set aside.

Cook **500g gnocchi** in the boiling water, according to the packet instructions, reserving 3–4 tbsp of the cooking water. Once drained, return the gnocchi to the empty pan and stir through the pesto and reserved cooking water, then spoon into bowls, grate over **some lemon zest** and squeeze over **some lemon juice** before serving.

Tip: If you don't have a food processor, bash the ingredients together in a pestle and mortar – or a makeshift one using a bowl and a rolling pin.

tomato, caper + raisin pasta

serves 4
ready in 25 minutes

Heat 1 tbsp oil in a saucepan, add **2 chopped garlic cloves, 60g raisins** and **2 tbsp drained capers**, and sizzle for 30 seconds. Tip in a **680g jar of tomato passata**, cover the pan leaving the lid a little ajar, and simmer gently for 15–20 minutes. Season and add a pinch of sugar if needed.

Meanwhile, cook **300g pasta** in a pan of boiling salted water, according to the packet instructions, then drain, tip into the pan of tomato sauce and stir through.

Spoon the pasta into bowls, scatter over **25g toasted pine nuts** and grate over a little **Parmesan cheese** before serving.

Tip: This sauce is great with pan-fried fish or chicken too.

chicken traybake sicilian-style

serves 4
ready in about 1 hour

Heat the oven to 200°C/180°C/gas mark 6. Roughly chop or crush **2 tsp fennel seeds**, then tip into a large roasting tray. Tear **200g sourdough bread** into chunks and add to the tray, along with **700g mixed tomatoes**, halved if large, **100g mixed olives**, **1 bulb of garlic**, cloves separated and lightly bashed, and 3 tbsp extra virgin olive oil. Season well and toss everything together.

Rub **4 large or 8 small chicken thighs** with a little olive oil and seasoning, then place on top of the vegetables and roast for 40–50 minutes, turning the vegetables halfway through, until the chicken is cooked through and the skin is crispy. Scatter over **50g rocket** before serving or serve alongside.

pizza alsace-style

serves 1–2
ready in 35 minutes

Heat the oven to 220°C/200°C fan/gas mark 7. Mix up a **145g packet of pizza base mix** according to the packet instructions, then roll out into a 25–30cm thin round, transfer to a lightly oiled baking tray and set aside for 10 minutes. Restretch a little if needed after resting.

Very thinly slice **3 chestnut mushrooms** and mix with 1 tsp olive oil and some seasoning. Spread **100g crème fraîche** over the pizza base, grate over **plenty of nutmeg**, then top with ½ **very thinly sliced small onion, 85g smoked lardons** and the mushrooms. Grind over some pepper, drizzle with a little olive oil and bake for 15–20 minutes until golden and bubbling.

Tip: You can use a ready-made pizza base or flatbread instead but reduce the cooking time by 5 minutes.

chermoula-grilled fish + minted couscous

serves 2
ready in 45 minutes

Rub **2 whole, scaled and gutted, mackerel (or fish of your choice)** all over with **2 tbsp chermoula paste** and some seasoning, not forgetting the inside, then chill for at least 30 minutes.

Cook **100g giant couscous** according to the packet instructions, then leave to cool a little.

Heat the grill to high. Transfer the mackerel to a baking tray, drizzle with a little olive oil and grill for 4–5 minutes on each side until cooked through.

Mix together 1½ tbsp extra virgin olive oil, the **zest and juice of 1 lemon**, **½ small bunch of mint**, roughly chopped and **25g roughly chopped dried cranberries or cherries** in a large bowl. Season well, tip in the cooled couscous and stir together. Serve with the grilled mackerel.

salmon baked in a parcel with rosemary butter

serves 4
ready in 35 minutes

Heat the oven to 200°C/180°C fan/gas mark 6. Toast **50g blanched hazelnuts** in the oven for 8 minutes, leave to cool, then roughly chop. Bring a pan of salted water to the boil.

Mash together 60g butter with the leaves from **2 sprigs of rosemary**, finely chopped, the hazelnuts and some seasoning.

Very thinly slice **2 bulbs of fennel** (reserving any leafy fronds) and divide between four large pieces of parchment paper. Top with **4 x 140g salmon fillets** and dot over the butter, then wrap up the parcels so they are well sealed, place on a tray and bake for 18–20 minutes.

Meanwhile, boil **600g baby potatoes** in the salted water for 15–20 minutes, or until tender.

Unwrap the parcels and serve the salmon and fennel with the potatoes, sprinkling over any fennel fronds.

tomato + lime chicken pickle curry

serves 2
ready in 30 minutes

Chop **4 skinless and boneless chicken thighs** into chunks, mix with **1 heaped tbsp lime pickle or curry paste** and chill for 15 minutes.

Meanwhile, thickly slice ¼ **cucumber**, then quarter each slice and warm **2 small naan breads** according to the packet instructions.

Heat 2 tsp oil in a non-stick frying pan over a medium–high heat and fry the chicken for 8–10 minutes until well-browned, stirring and scraping the bottom of the pan as it cooks. Reduce the heat a little, add **200g halved cherry tomatoes** and cook for 3 minutes, or until softened, then stir in ½ tsp sugar, another 1 tbsp lime pickle or curry paste and cook for 2–3 minutes until sizzling and the chicken is cooked through.

Serve with the cucumber, warm naan and a **dollop of Greek yogurt**.

thai butter-roasted chicken with radish + avocado salad

serves 2
ready in 25 minutes

Heat the oven to 200°C/180°C fan/gas mark 6. Mash together **4 tsp Thai green curry paste** and 25g softened butter, then slash the tops of **2 skinless and boneless chicken breasts** and rub the butter all over.

Place the chicken in a small baking dish and roast for 20–25 minutes, basting halfway through, until the juices run clear and the topping is lightly browned.

Meanwhile, chop **1 large avocado** into cubes and mix with **85g grated radishes** and a **small bunch of roughly chopped coriander**.

Toast **2–3 heaped tbsp desiccated coconut** in a dry frying pan over a low heat until lightly browned. Slice the chicken and divide it between plates with the salad. Drizzle over the cooking juices and sprinkle with the coconut.

naked gyoza + wasabi guacamole

serves 4
ready in 25 minutes

In a bowl, mix together **500g lean pork mince**, a **3cm knob of ginger**, peeled and grated, **4 finely chopped spring onions**, **3 tbsp teriyaki sauce or thick sweet soy sauce** and some seasoning, then shape into 20 small patties.

Heat a drizzle of oil in a large non-stick frying pan over a high heat and brown the patties for 2 minutes on each side (cooking in batches if your pan isn't big enough). Lower the heat a little, add 2 tbsp boiling water to the pan, cover and cook for 5 minutes until cooked through.

Mash the flesh of **2 avocados** with **2 tsp wasabi paste or strong horseradish cream** and seasoning.

Heat **2 x 250g packets of microwavable coconut rice** according to the packet instructions. Serve the patties with the rice and guacamole. Drizzle over the pan juices, sprinkle with **2 finely shredded spring onions** and serve extra teriyaki or thick sweet soy sauce on the side.

crispy noodle cake + hoisin aubergines

serves 2
ready in 30 minutes

Cook **125g medium egg noodles** according to the packet instructions, drain and set aside. Heat 2 tbsp oil in a large non-stick frying pan over a high heat, add half the noodles and cook for about 3 minutes until brown and really crispy on the bottom, then flip over and cook the other side. Repeat with more oil and the remaining noodles. Remove and set aside.

Meanwhile, bring a pan of water to the boil and set a steamer over the top. Cut **2 small aubergines** into chunky chips and steam for 5–8 minutes until tender.

Heat 2 more tbsp oil in the frying pan over a high heat. Add the aubergine and stir-fry for 5–8 minutes until browned. Add a **2.5cm knob of ginger**, peeled and cut into matchsticks, ¾ **finely sliced deseeded red chilli** and most of a **bunch of spring onions**, finely sliced at an angle. Fry for 1–2 minutes, then stir through **4 tbsp hoisin or thick sweet soy sauce** and let it bubble.

Pile the aubergines onto the noodle cakes and top with the remaining sliced spring onions and chilli.

mustard pork with cider + caramelised apples

serves 3
ready in 25 minutes

Slice **450–500g pork tenderloin** into 2cm thick slices. Tip 4 tbsp plain flour into a bowl, season, add the pork and toss together.

Heat 1 tbsp olive oil in a large non-stick frying pan over a high heat. Shake any excess flour from the pork, then fry for 2–3 minutes on each side until browned, then remove and set aside.

Add another 1 tbsp oil to the pan and cook **2 sliced onions** for 5 minutes, stirring, until golden brown. Core **2 apples**, slice into thin wedges, add to the pan with a drizzle of oil and cook for 5 minutes until caramelised. Stir in **175ml cider**, **1½ tbsp wholegrain mustard** and season.

Return the pork to the pan, cover and simmer gently for 3–4 minutes until the pork is just cooked. Serve with **200g shredded savoy cabbage or greens**, steamed or boiled under tender.

cumin lamb
with watercress
+ feta sauce

serves 4
ready in 30 minutes

Mix **2 tsp roughly chopped cumin seeds**, 2 tbsp olive oil and some seasoning together in a bowl. Add **4 lamb leg steaks (about 150g each)** and mix until coated, then set aside.

Bring a pan of salted water to the boil, drop in **500g baby potatoes** and boil for 15 minutes, or until tender, then drain and set aside.

Heat a large frying pan and cook the lamb over a high heat for 3–4 minutes on each side, depending on thickness, then leave to rest.

Place **90g watercress**, **100g roughly broken feta cheese** and **2 tbsp lemon juice** with 1–2 tbsp cold water and some seasoning in a food processor, and whiz together until smooth.

Slice the lamb and serve with the potatoes, sauce and a **few extra watercress leaves** to garnish.

griddled steak with red onions, beans + pesto

serves 2
ready in 15 minutes

Rub **2 x 200g rump or your favourite steak** all over with a little olive oil and season. Heat a griddle or frying pan over a high heat and, when hot, add the steaks and cook for 2–3 minutes on each side for medium rare, depending on thickness, then remove from the pan and set aside to rest. Slice **1 red onion** into 6 wedges, add to the pan and cook for 5 minutes, turning until charred all over.

Meanwhile, drain and rinse a **400g tin of mixed beans**. Tip into a saucepan with 1 tbsp cold water and heat for 3–4 minutes, then stir through **2½ tbsp pesto** (fresh if possible), 1 tbsp cold water and some seasoning, and warm through.

Slice the steak and serve with the beans, onion and **a handful of rocket leaves**.

smoked sausage + red cabbage hash

serves 4
ready in 30 minutes

Bring a large pan of salted water to the boil. Cut **750g potatoes** into 2cm dice and simmer for 10 minutes, or until tender, then drain.

Heat 35g butter in a large non-stick frying pan, add **1 sliced onion** and **200g sliced smoked sausage** and cook for 8 minutes until browned. Tip in the potatoes and cook for a further 8–10 minutes until crispy.

Meanwhile, bring a large pan of water to the boil, add a splash of vinegar and very gently stir the water. Crack **2 eggs** into two separate small bowls and carefully slide each egg into the simmering water. Lightly poach the eggs for 3–4 minutes, then remove with a slotted spoon and drain. Repeat with a further **2 eggs**.

Stir **1 tsp caraway seeds** and some seasoning through the potato mix and cook for 2 minutes more, then push the potato to the side of the pan and spoon in a **200g jar of German-style red cabbage in vinegar, drained**. Once warmed, gently fold all the ingredients together and serve topped with the poached eggs and some black pepper.

3.
DESSERTS + SNACKS

orange + passion fruit carpaccio

serves 4
ready in 15 minutes

Scoop the seeds and pulp from **2 ripe passion fruit** into a small saucepan. Add **2 tbsp runny honey** and 1 tbsp cold water, bring to the boil, then turn down the heat and simmer gently for 2 minutes until syrupy. Set aside to cool.

Using a sharp knife, cut the bottoms and tops off **4 oranges**, then work the knife down the sides from top to bottom to remove the rind. Thinly slice each orange into rounds and arrange on a serving plate, then pour the passion fruit syrup over the top and chill until ready to eat.

Grate over the **zest of 1 lime** and squeeze over **a little lime juice** before serving.

blackberry + plum meringue crush

serves 4
ready in 30 minutes

Chop **4 ripe plums** into eighths and place in a small saucepan. Sprinkle over 2 tbsp caster sugar and 2 tbsp cold water and bubble gently for 5 minutes until the fruit is soft, juicy and syrupy but still holding its shape. Taste and add more sugar if needed, then take off the heat, stir through **150g blackberries** and set aside to cool completely.

When ready to serve, pour **300ml double cream**, **200g Greek yogurt** and **¼ tsp rosewater** into a bowl and whisk until just holding its shape. Divide between four bowls and crush over **4 mini meringues**, then lightly stir the fruit and spoon over the top, rippling the juices through the cream.

Tip: If you can't find mini meringues, use 4–6 meringue nests.

summer fruit compote + white chocolate sauce

serves 4–6
ready in 30 minutes

Tip **500g mixed summer berries** (blueberries, raspberries and halved strawberries) into a pan with 1–2 tbsp caster sugar and 2 tbsp cold water, stir gently, then set over a low heat. Bring to a simmer and cook for 2–3 minutes until the fruits are just beginning to release their juices but are still holding their shape, then set aside to cool.

Meanwhile, very gently heat **150ml double cream** with **7 lightly bashed cardamom pods** and, just before it starts to simmer, take off the heat and leave to infuse for 15 minutes. Remove the cardamom pods, add **100g finely chopped good-quality white chocolate** and return to a very low heat, stirring gently until smooth.

Spoon the sauce into shallow bowls, top with the warm fruit and drizzle over the juices.

Tip: The cardamom in this recipe is quite subtle. For a more pronounced flavour, leave to infuse for longer.

banana, chocolate + hazelnut strudel

serves 6
ready in 45 minutes

Heat the oven to 200°C/180°C fan/gas mark 6 and place a tray inside.

Melt 50g butter and brush over **6 sheets of filo pastry**, layering the sheets on top of each other, butter-side up. Gently spread **200g chocolate hazelnut spread** all over the top sheet, leaving a border around the edges, then sprinkle over **50g toasted chopped hazelnuts**, reserving a small handful for the top.

Roughly chop **5 medium bananas** and pile down the centre of the pastry, then fold the sides and the ends over to enclose and flip onto a piece of baking parchment, seam-side down. Brush with more melted butter, then lift onto the hot baking tray, sprinkle with the nuts and bake for 30 minutes until golden brown. Dust with **icing sugar** before serving with **cream or ice cream**.

chocolate orange + avocado mousse

serves 4
ready in 40 minutes

Melt **100g 70% dark chocolate** in the microwave (stirring every 10 seconds), or in a bowl over a pan of simmering water, then leave to cool.

Scoop the flesh from **2 medium ripe avocados** and place in the bowl of a food processor (or use a hand blender and a bowl). Add **4–5 tbsp runny honey**, **most of the zest from 1 orange** and **3 tbsp orange juice**, and blend until smooth. Transfer to a bowl, pour in the cooled chocolate and stir to combine.

Spoon the mousse into serving dishes and chill for 20 minutes, then grate over a **little extra chocolate** and sprinkle with the remaining **orange zest** before serving.

chocolate +
coconut
rum tarts

makes 6
ready in 50 minutes

Heat the oven to 180˚C/160˚C fan/gas mark 4. Use a rolling pin to roll out **6 large coconut macaroon biscuits** until very thin, then push gently into a 6-hole muffin tin, patching up any holes – it will look rustic. Bake for 8 minutes, then leave to cool in the tins.

Finely chop **200g 70% dark chocolate** and place in a jug, keeping back a few squares for decoration. Heat **200ml coconut milk** in a pan and, just before it comes to the boil, pour it over the chopped chocolate. Leave for 5 minutes, then add **2½ tbsp dark rum** and stir until melted and smooth.

Pour the filling into the macaroon cases and leave to cool, then chill until firm for about 20 minutes (use a table knife to release them from the tin if needed). Shave or grate the reserved chocolate over the tarts before serving.

Tip: If the chocolate hasn't melted completely in the coconut milk, microwave for 10 seconds at a time. To speed up the chilling, pop the tarts in the freezer.

affogato

serves 4
ready in 10 minutes

Scoop **4 balls of good-quality vanilla ice cream** into 4 glasses or small bowls and place the glasses or bowls in the freezer.

When ready to serve, make up **4 shots of strong espresso coffee**, then pour over the ice cream and crumble **4 cantucci or biscotti biscuits** on top. Serve with an extra biscuit or two on the side.

Tip: Make it a dessert fit for a dinner party by adding a shot of amaretto or Kahlua to the coffee.

strawberry tart

serves 6–8
ready in 45 minutes

Heat the oven to 200°C/180°C fan/gas mark 6. Unroll **320g ready-rolled sweet shortcrust pastry** and transfer to a baking tray. Prick the pastry all over with a fork, bake for 12–15 minutes until golden brown, then leave to cool.

Meanwhile, cut the tops off **450g strawberries**, then slice thinly and layer in rows over the pastry base, leaving a 1cm border around the edge.

Gently heat **2 tbsp redcurrant jelly** in a small pan and, when melted, use a brush to dab the glaze over the strawberries. Set aside for 10 minutes, then slice and serve with **dollops of thick cream**.

blueberry + lemon muffins

makes 12
ready in 40 minutes

Heat the oven to 180°C/160°C fan/gas mark 4. Line a 12-hole muffin tin with cases.

Tip **300g self-raising flour**, **200g golden caster sugar**, the **zest of 1 large lemon** and 1 tsp salt into a large bowl. In another bowl, beat together **2 eggs**, 150ml milk and 100ml sunflower oil. Pour the wet mixture into the flour and lightly stir until just combined – don't overmix.

Gently swirl **200g blueberries** through the mix, then divide between the cases and bake for 25–28 minutes until golden and a skewer inserted into the centre comes out clean.

Mix **1½ tbsp golden caster sugar** with **1½ tbsp lemon juice** until dissolved, then brush or spoon over the hot muffins. Cool in the tin for 5 minutes, then transfer to a wire rack to cool completely.

no-cook
chocolate cake

makes 15–20 slices
ready in 35 minutes

Grease and roughly line a 18–20cm round or square tin, container or Tupperware box with baking parchment.

Melt 100g butter, **2 tbsp honey**, and **300g chopped 70% dark chocolate** together in a small pan, stirring until smooth. Add **150g ginger biscuits**, bashed into small chunks, **50g roughly chopped pistachio nuts** and **75g roughly chopped glacé cherries** and stir to combine, then tip into the tin.

Using the back of a spoon, spread the mixture out, pushing down firmly and well into the corners. Pop into the freezer for 20 minutes or chill for 45 minutes in the fridge until very firm. Dust with **icing sugar** and cut into wedges or squares.

peanut butter + chocolate biscuits

makes 18
ready in 30 minutes

Heat the oven to 180°C/160°C fan/gas mark 4. Beat **200g crunchy peanut butter, 150g soft light brown sugar, 1 lightly beaten egg** and a pinch of salt together in a bowl.

Shape the dough into walnut-sized balls (about 1 tbsp mixture each) and space out on a parchment-lined baking tray. Flatten slightly with the back of a fork and bake for 10–12 minutes until golden brown. Cool on the tray for 5 minutes, then transfer to a wire rack.

Melt **50g dark chocolate** in the microwave (stirring every 10 seconds), or in a bowl over a pan of simmering water, then drizzle over the cool biscuits. Leave to set, then serve.

salted caramel popcorn

serves 6–8
ready in 20 minutes

Pour 2 tbsp oil into a large saucepan along with **2 popping corn kernels**, then cover and heat over a medium–high heat until the kernels pop. Lift the lid, add **100g corn kernels**, cover again and, holding the lid on, shake the pan. Cook until you can no longer hear any popping, then tip into a very large bowl.

Cool the pan under cold water, then clean. Add 150g caster sugar and 3 tbsp cold water and heat gently without stirring until the sugar has dissolved, then increase the heat and let it bubble until it turns a deep golden honey colour. Add 75g butter and 2 tsp salt, then swirl until melted. Remove from the heat, spoon in **1 tsp bicarbonate of soda** and stir using an oiled spatula. Pour the salted caramel over the popcorn and stir well again, then tip onto a parchment-lined baking tray and leave to cool.

Tip: Be very careful when making this as the hot caramel can easily burn.

rosemary + honey roast nuts

serves 4–6 as a nibble
ready in 20 minutes

Heat the oven to 200°C/180°C fan/gas mark 6. In a large bowl, place **200g mixed unsalted nuts** with 2 tsp extra virgin olive oil, ¾ tsp sea salt, **2 sprigs of rosemary**, leaves finely chopped, **2 tbsp runny honey** and a **pinch of chilli flakes** and mix well.

Spread the nuts out on a parchment-lined baking tray and roast for 10 minutes, then give everything a stir and cook for a further 4–5 minutes until golden. Leave to cool on the tray before transferring to a bowl to serve. Sprinkle with a little more salt if needed.

marinated olives
+ manchego

makes 1 large jar
ready in 30 minutes

Heat **1 tsp fennel seeds** in a dry frying pan until fragrant. Add the peeled rind from ½ **orange**, **2 bashed garlic cloves** and the leaves from **5 large thyme sprigs** and heat for 1 minute, then pour in 75ml extra virgin olive oil and **1½ tbsp orange juice**. Add **300g drained and rinsed black and green olives** and gently warm through.

Tip the olives into a bowl or jar and leave to cool, then stir through **50g cubed manchego cheese**. Eat straight away or leave to marinate in the fridge for a few hours or up to one week (even better!), but bring to room temperature before serving.

paprika chips + white bean dip

serves 4–6
ready in 20 minutes

Heat the oven to 200°C/180°C fan/gas mark 6. Cut **4 pitta breads** into rough triangles, then separate each triangle into its two halves. Arrange on two baking trays, then drizzle with 3 tbsp olive oil and sprinkle over ½ **tsp sweet smoked paprika** and a pinch of sea salt. Bake for 8–10 minutes until golden and crisp, then leave to cool.

Meanwhile, drain a **400g tin of cannellini beans** and tip into a bowl with **1 crushed garlic clove**, **5 tbsp Greek yogurt**, **4 tsp lemon juice**, 1 tbsp extra virgin olive oil and some seasoning. Mash together until smooth.

Tip the dip into a bowl, drizzle with olive oil and scatter over a **handful of chopped parsley**. Serve with the pitta crisps.

beef, olive + tomato parcels

makes 12
ready in 40 minutes

Heat the oven to 200°C/180°C fan/gas mark 6. Slit the skins of **6 beef sausages (about 400g)** and tip the meat into a bowl, discarding the skins. Add **50g sundried tomatoes**, finely chopped, **50g pitted mixed olives**, sliced, and a little seasoning and mix well, then shape the meat into 12 sausages.

Halve **6 sheets of filo pastry** lengthways to make 12 sheets. Place a sausage next to the short edge of each piece, then roll over once, fold in the sides and continue rolling into a parcel.

Transfer the parcels to a greased baking tray, brush generously with 25g melted butter, sprinkle with **1 tbsp dried oregano** and bake for 20–25 minutes until golden brown.

sunblushed foccacia

makes 1 large loaf
ready in about 1 hour

Mix a **500g packet of ciabatta bread mix** according to the packet instructions.

Generously oil a 15 x 30cm deep baking dish and sprinkle the leaves of **2 sprigs of rosemary** over the base.

Turn out the dough and shape into a rough rectangle, then lift into the dish and push well into the corners so that it fills the tray. Cover with a damp cloth and leave in a warm place for 30 minutes, or until doubled in size. Heat the oven to 230°C/210°C fan/gas mark 8.

Poke **250g mixed antipasti** and the leaves from **2–3 sprigs of rosemary** into the top of the dough. Drizzle over 1–2 tbsp extra virgin olive oil and 1 tsp sea salt flakes and bake for 20–25 minutes until golden brown. Leave to cool a little before slicing and serving.

cheese + poppy seed biscuits

makes 18–20
ready in 45 minutes

Heat the oven to 180°C/160°C fan/gas mark 4. Place **75g plain flour**, **75g finely grated Cheddar or strong hard cheese**, **1 tsp English or French mustard**, **a good pinch of cayenne pepper**, a pinch salt and a grinding of black pepper into a bowl and mix well. Add 50g cold cubed butter and rub with your fingertips until evenly distributed and a dough starts to form. Knead a little, then shape into a log about 13cm long.

Place **1 heaped tbsp poppy seeds** on a large plate and roll the log in it until completely coated, then wrap in clingfilm and freeze for 15 minutes.

Slice the log into 0.5cm rounds and space well apart on a parchment paper-lined baking tray. Bake for 15–18 minutes until golden, then leave to cool.

Tip: To speed things up, tip all the ingredients, except the poppy seeds, into a food processor and blitz until a dough is formed, then roll into a log and freeze.

INDEX

THANK YOU

To everyone at Kyle Books for making this book possible, a wonderful experience and so good-looking, especially my amazing editor Vicki Murrell, Judith Hannam, Kyle Cathie, Corinne Maasciocchi, Victoria Scales, Nic Jones and Gemma John.

I'm hugely grateful to Louise Hagger, whose photography is stunning – Louise, I have so much respect for your work. To Alexander Breeze, for his beautiful prop styling, creative ideas and for always going the extra mile – that egg purse is fantastic! It was so much fun photographing the book with you both. To designer Caroline Clark, for making the book look so good.

To my family and friends, for supporting me throughout the writing of this book, and always, and for being my chief tasters. Especially my parents Charles and Christine, sisters Anna and Sophie and their husbands Gary and Phil. Thank you too to Janet, Abigail, Nic, Jill, Rosalie and Rachel. To my greyhound Pearl for keeping me company whilst I was recipe writing, and for polishing off any testing leftovers.

Tom, my best friend, thank you for believing in me.